Princess September

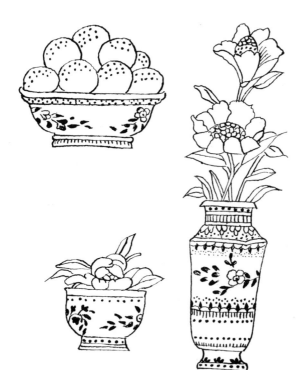

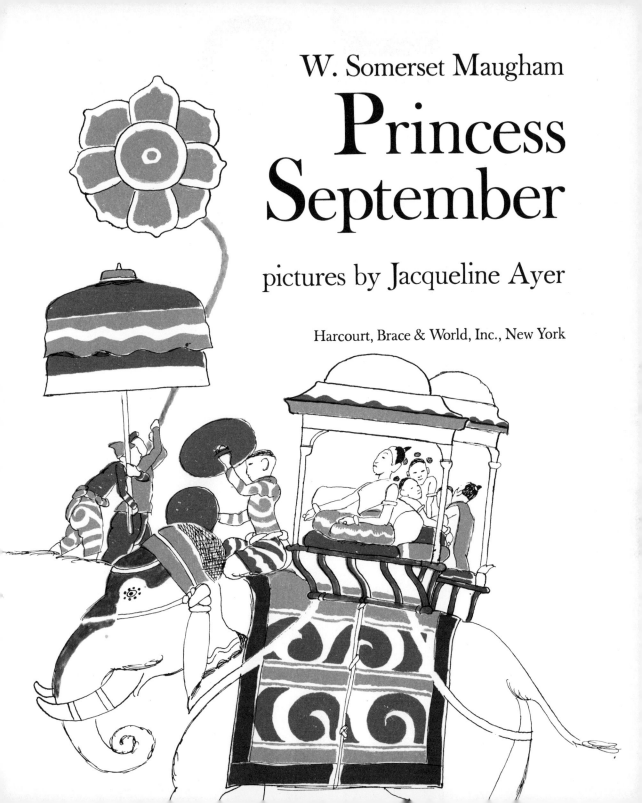

W. Somerset Maugham
Princess
September

pictures by Jacqueline Ayer

Harcourt, Brace & World, Inc., New York

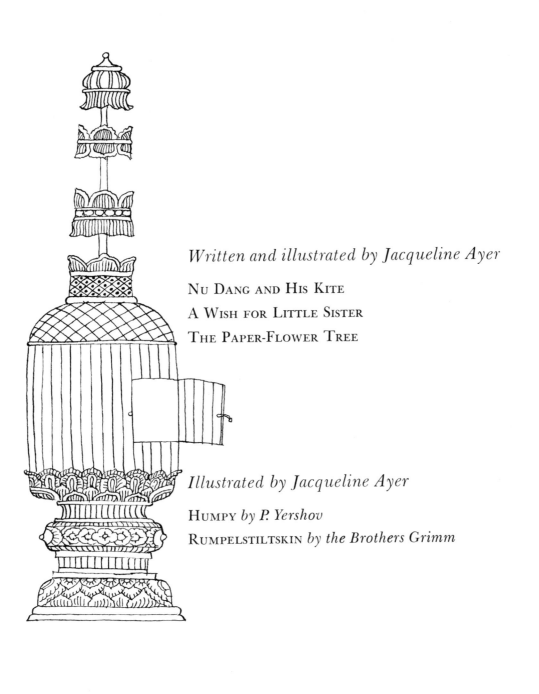

Written and illustrated by Jacqueline Ayer

Nu Dang and His Kite
A Wish for Little Sister
The Paper-Flower Tree

Illustrated by Jacqueline Ayer

Humpy by P. Yershov
Rumpelstiltskin by the Brothers Grimm

FIRST the King of Siam had two daughters, and he called them Night and Day. Then he had two more, so he changed the names of the first ones and called the four of them after the seasons, Spring and Autumn, Winter and Summer. But in course of time he had three others, and he changed their names again and called all seven by the days of the week. But when his eighth daughter was born he did not know what to do till he suddenly thought of the months of the year. The Queen

said there were only twelve and it confused her to have to remember so many new names, but the King had a methodical mind and when he made it up he never could change it if he tried. He changed the names of all his daughters and called them January, February, March (though of course in Siamese), till he came to the youngest, who was called August, and the next one was called September.

"That only leaves October, November, and December," said the Queen. "And after that we shall have to begin all over again."

"No, we shan't," said the King, "because I think twelve daughters are enough for any man, and after the birth of dear little December I shall be reluctantly compelled to cut off your head."

He cried bitterly when he said this, for he was extremely fond of the Queen. Of course it made the Queen very uneasy, because she knew that it would distress the King very much if he had to cut off her head. And it would not be very nice for her. But it so happened that there was no need for either of them to worry, because September was the last daughter they ever had. The Queen only had sons after that, and they were called by the letters of the alphabet, so there was no cause for anxiety there for a long time, since she had only reached the letter J.

Now the King of Siam's daughters had had their characters permanently embittered by having to change their names in this way, and the older ones, whose names of course had been changed oftener than the others, had their characters more permanently embittered. But September, who had never known what it was to be called anything but September (except of course by her sisters, who, because their characters were embittered, called her all sorts of names), had a very sweet and charming nature.

The King of Siam had a habit which I think might be usefully imitated in Europe. Instead of receiving presents on his birthday he gave them, and it looks as though he liked it, for he used often to say he was sorry he had only been born on one day and so only had one birthday in the year. But in this way he managed in course of time to give away all his wedding presents, and the loyal addresses which the mayors of the cities in Siam presented him with, and all his old crowns which had gone out of fashion. One year on his birthday, not

having anything else handy, he gave each of his daughters a beautiful green parrot in a beautiful golden cage. There were nine of them, and on each cage was written the name of the month which was the name of the Princess it belonged to. The nine Princesses were very proud of their parrots, and they spent an hour every day (for, like their father, they were of a methodical turn of mind) in teaching them to talk. Presently all the parrots could say God save the King (in Siamese, which is very difficult), and some of them could say Pretty Polly in no less than seven Oriental languages. But one day when the Princess September went to say good morning to her parrot, she found it lying

dead at the bottom of its golden cage. She burst into a flood of tears, and nothing that her maids of honor could say comforted her. She cried so much that the maids of honor, not knowing what to do, told the Queen, and the Queen said it was stuff and nonsense and the child had better go to bed without any supper. The maids of honor wanted to go to a party, so they put the Princess September to bed as quickly

as they could and left her by herself. And while she lay in her bed, crying still, even though she felt rather hungry, she saw a little bird hop into her room. She took her thumb out of her mouth and sat up. Then the little bird began to sing, and he sang a beautiful song all about the lake in the King's garden, and the willow trees that looked at themselves in the still water, and the goldfish that glided in and out of the branches that were reflected in it. When he had finished, the Princess was not crying any more and she quite forgot that she had had no supper.

"That was a very nice song," she said.

The little bird gave her a bow, for artistes have naturally good manners and they like to be appreciated.

"Would you care to have me instead of your parrot?" said the little bird. "It's true that I'm not so pretty to look at, but, on the other hand, I have a much better voice."

The Princess September clapped her hands with delight, and then the little bird hopped onto the end of her bed and sang her to sleep.

When she awoke next day the little bird was still sitting there, and as she opened her eyes he said, "Good morning." The maids of honor brought in her breakfast, and he ate rice out of her hand, and he had his bath in her saucer. He drank out of it, too. The maids of honor said they didn't think it was very polite to drink one's bath water, but the Princess September said that was the artistic temperament. When he had finished his breakfast he began to sing again so beautifully that the maids of honor were quite surprised, for they had never heard anything like it, and the Princess September was very proud and happy.

"Now I want to show you to my eight sisters," said the Princess.

She stretched out the first finger of her right hand so that it served as a perch, and the little bird flew down and sat on it. Then, followed by her maids of honor, she went through the palace and called on each of the Princesses in turn, starting with January, for she was mindful of etiquette, and going all the way down to August. And for each of the Princesses the little bird sang a different song. But the parrots could only say God save the King and Pretty Polly. At last she showed the little bird to the King and Queen. They were surprised and delighted.

"I knew I was right to send you to bed without any supper," said the Queen.

"This bird sings much better than the parrots," said the King.

"I should have thought you got quite tired of hearing people say 'God save the King,'" said the Queen. "I can't think why those girls wanted to teach their parrots to say it too."

"The sentiment is admirable," said the King, "and I never mind how often I hear it. But I do get tired of hearing those parrots say 'Pretty Polly.'"

"They say it in seven different languages," said the Princesses.

"I dare say they do," said the King, "but it reminds me too much

of my councillors. They say the same thing in seven different ways, and it never means anything in any way they say it."

The Princesses, their characters (as I have already said) being naturally embittered, were vexed at this, and the parrots looked very glum indeed. But the Princess September ran through all the rooms of the palace, singing like a lark, while the little bird flew round and round her, singing like a nightingale, which indeed it was.

Things went on like this for several days, and then the eight Princesses put their heads together. They went to September and sat down in a circle round her, hiding their feet as it is proper for Siamese Princesses to do.

"My poor September," they said, "we are so sorry for the death of

your beautiful parrot. It must be dreadful for you not to have a pet bird as we have. So we have put all our pocket money together, and we are going to buy you a lovely green and yellow parrot."

"Thank you for nothing," said September. (This was not very civil of her, but Siamese Princesses are sometimes a little short with one another.) "I have a pet bird which sings the most charming songs to me, and I don't know what on earth I should do with a green and yellow parrot."

January sniffed, then February sniffed, then March sniffed; in fact, all the Princesses sniffed, but in their proper order of precedence. When they had finished September asked them:

"Why do you sniff? Have you all got colds in the head?"

"Well, my dear," they said, "it's absurd to talk of *your* bird when the little fellow flies in and out just as he likes." They looked round the room and raised their eyebrows so high that their foreheads entirely disappeared.

"You'll get dreadful wrinkles," said September.

"Do you mind our asking where your bird is now?" they said.

"He's gone to pay a visit to his father-in-law," said the Princess September.

"And what makes you think he'll come back?" asked the Princesses.

"He always does come back," said September.

"Well, my dear," said the eight Princesses, "if you'll take our advice, you won't run any risks like that. If he comes back—and, mind you, if he does you'll be lucky—pop him into the cage and keep him there. That's the only way you can be sure of him."

"But I like to have him fly about the room," said the Princess September.

"Safety first," said her sisters ominously.

They got up and walked out of the room, shaking their heads, and they left September very uneasy. It seemed to her that her little bird was away a long time, and she could not think what he was doing. Something might have happened to him. What with hawks and men with snares, you never knew what trouble he might get into. Besides, he might forget her, or he might take a fancy to somebody else—that would be dreadful; oh, she wished he were safely back again and in the golden cage that stood there empty and ready. For when the maids of honor had buried the dead parrot they had left the cage in its old place.

Suddenly September heard a tweet-tweet just behind her ear, and she saw the little bird sitting on her shoulder. He had come in so quietly and alighted so softly that she had not heard him.

"I wondered what on earth had become of you," said the Princess.

"I thought you'd wonder that," said the little bird. "The fact is I very nearly didn't come back tonight at all. My father-in-law was giving a party, and they all wanted me to stay, but I thought you'd be anxious."

Under the circumstances, this was a very unfortunate remark for the little bird to make.

September felt her heart go thump, thump against her chest, and she made up her mind to take no more risks. She put up her hand and took hold of the bird. This he was quite used to—she liked feeling his heart go pit-a-pat, so fast, in the hollow of her hand, and I think he liked the soft warmth of her little hand. So the bird suspected nothing, and he was so surprised when she carried him over to the cage, popped him in, and shut the door on him that for a moment he could think of nothing to say. But in a moment or two he hopped up on the ivory perch and said:

"What is the joke?"

"There's no joke," said September, "but some of Mama's cats are prowling about tonight, and I think you're much safer in there."

"I can't think why the Queen wants to have all those cats," said the little bird, rather crossly.

"Well, you see, they're very special cats," said the Princess. "They have blue eyes and a kink in their tails, and they're a speciality of the Royal Family, if you understand what I mean."

"Perfectly," said the little bird, "but why did you put me in this cage without saying anything about it? I don't think it's the sort of place I like."

"I shouldn't have slept a wink all night if I hadn't known you were safe."

"Well, just for this once I don't mind," said the little bird, "so long as you let me out in the morning."

He ate a very good supper and then began to sing. But in the middle of his song he stopped.

"I don't know what is the matter with me," he said, "but I don't feel like singing tonight."

"Very well," said September, "go to sleep instead."

So he put his head under his wing and in a minute was fast asleep. September went to sleep, too. But when the dawn broke she was awakened by the little bird calling her at the top of his voice.

"Wake up, wake up," he said. "Open the door of this cage and let me out. I want to have a good fly while the dew is still on the ground."

"You're much better off where you are," said September. "You have a beautiful golden cage. It was made by the best workman in my papa's kingdom, and my papa was so pleased with it that he cut off his head so that he should never make another."

"Let me out, let me out," said the little bird.

"You'll have three meals a day served by my maids of honor; you'll have nothing to worry you from morning till night, and you can sing to your heart's content."

"Let me out, let me out," said the little bird. And he tried to slip through the bars of the cage, but of course he couldn't, and he beat against the door, but of course he couldn't open it. Then the eight

Princesses came in and looked at him. They told September she was very wise to take their advice. They said he would soon get used to the cage and in a few days would quite forget that he had ever been free. The little bird said nothing at all while they were there, but as soon as they were gone he began to cry again: "Let me out, let me out."

"Don't be such an old silly," said September. "I've only put you in the cage because I'm so fond of you. *I* know what's good for you much better than you do yourself. Sing me a little song and I'll give you a piece of brown sugar."

But the little bird stood in the corner of his cage, looking out at the blue sky, and never sang a note. He never sang all day.

"What's the good of sulking?" said September. "Why don't you sing and forget your troubles?"

"How can I sing?" answered the bird. "I want to see the trees and the lake and the green rice growing in the fields."

"If that's all you want, I'll take you for a walk," said September.

She picked up the cage and went out, and she walked down to the lake round which grew the willow trees, and she stood at the edge of the rice fields that stretched as far as the eye could see.

"I'll take you out every day," she said. "I love you and I only want to make you happy."

"It's not the same thing," said the little bird. "The rice fields and the lake and the willow trees look quite different when you see them through the bars of a cage."

So she brought him home again and gave him his supper. But he wouldn't eat a thing. The Princess was a little anxious at this and asked her sisters what they thought about it.

"You must be firm," they said.

"But if he won't eat he'll die," she answered.

"That would be very ungrateful of him," they said. "He must know that you're only thinking of his own good. If he's obstinate and dies, it'll serve him right, and you'll be well rid of him."

September didn't see how that was going to do *her* very much good, but they were eight to one and all older than she, so she said nothing.

"Perhaps he'll have got used to his cage by tomorrow," she said.

And next day when she awoke she cried out good morning in a cheerful voice. She got no answer. She jumped out of bed and ran to the cage. She gave a startled cry, for there the little bird lay, at the bottom, on his side, with his eyes closed, and he looked as if he were dead. She opened the door and, putting her hand in, lifted him out. She gave a sob of relief, for she felt that his little heart was beating still.

"Wake up, wake up, little bird," she said.

She began to cry and her tears fell on the little bird. He opened his eyes and felt that the bars of the cage were no longer round him.

"I cannot sing unless I'm free, and if I cannot sing I die," he said.

The Princess gave a great sob.

"Then take your freedom," she said. "I shut you in a golden cage because I loved you and wanted to have you all to myself. But I never knew it would kill you. Go. Fly away among the trees that are round the lake and fly over the green rice fields. I love you enough to let you be happy in your own way."

She threw open the window and gently placed the little bird on the sill. He shook himself a little.

"Come and go as you will, little bird," she said. "I will never put you in a cage any more."

"I will come because I love you, little Princess," said the bird. "And I will sing you the loveliest songs I know. I shall go far away, but I

shall always come back, and I shall never forget you." He gave himself another shake. "Good gracious me, how stiff I am," he said.

Then he opened his wings and flew right away into the blue. But the little Princess burst into tears, for it is very difficult to put the happiness of someone you love before your own, and with her little bird far out of sight she felt on a sudden very lonely. When her sisters knew what had happened, they mocked her and said that the little bird

would never return. But he did at last. And he sat on September's shoulder and ate out of her hand and sang her the beautiful songs he had learned while he was flying up and down the fair places of the world. September kept her window open day and night so that the little bird might come into her room whenever he felt inclined, and this was very good for her; so she grew extremely beautiful. And when she was old enough she married the King of Cambodia and was carried all the way to the city in which he lived on a white elephant. But her sisters never slept with their windows open, so they grew extremely ugly as well as disagreeable, and when the time came to marry them off they were given away to the King's councillors with a pound of tea and a Siamese cat.